BEST FRIENDS
SLEEP OVER

For Diane

Library of Congress Cataloging-in-Publication Data

Rogers, Jacqueline.
  Best friends sleep over / by Jacqueline Rogers.
    p.   cm.
  Summary: Although he is somewhat scared, with a little help from his friends, Gilbert Gorilla
enjoys his first sleepover.
  ISBN 0-590-44793-9
  [1. Sleepovers—Fiction.   2. Friendship—Fiction.   3. Animals—Fiction.]   I. Title.
PZ7.R63545Be   1993
[E]—dc20   92-56895
                                                                                          CIP
                                                                                          AC

12 11 10 9 8 7 6 5 4 3 2 1   3 4 5 6 7 8/9

Printed in the U.S.A.   37

First Scholastic printing, October 1993

BEST FRIENDS
SLEEP OVER

by Jacqueline Rogers

SCHOLASTIC
HARDCOVER

SCHOLASTIC INC.
New York

Gilbert was invited to a slumber party at Eddie Bellows' house. Their best friends from school would be there — Ricky Rhino and Conner Crocodile. But Gilbert had never slept over at anyone's house before. As his mother helped him pack, he was excited, and a little worried.

"Everything at Eddie's is huge," Gilbert said to his mom.
"What if I can't find the bathroom in the dark tonight?"
"Don't worry," she said. "Your friends will help you."
"But what if I can't fall asleep without my good-night song?"
"Just remember to pack Clarence, your clown,"
said his mother. "He'll take my place and you'll be fine."

Gilbert's mother dropped him off at Eddie's
house. And by the time the four friends
greeted each other, Gilbert had forgotten
all his worries.

First Mrs. Bellows brought out a huge box of funny old clothes and costumes. When the boys grew tired of dressing up…

they played with Eddie's racetrack and cars. Ricky made
a bridge for the cars to go under, and Gilbert had to try it out.

Gilbert was "it" during Hide-and-Seek…

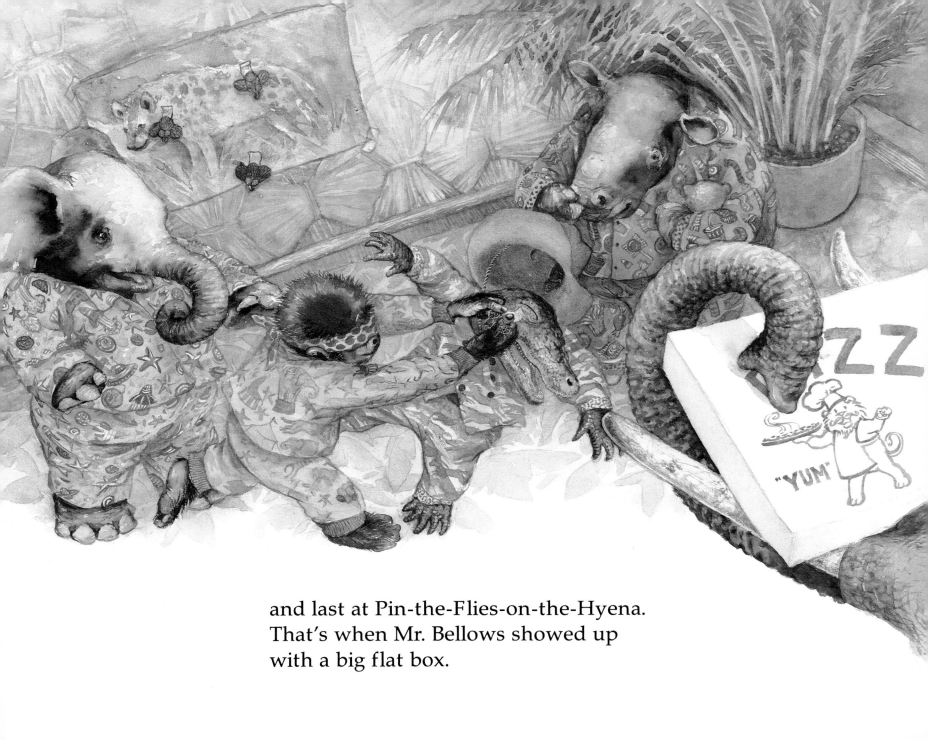

and last at Pin-the-Flies-on-the-Hyena.
That's when Mr. Bellows showed up
with a big flat box.

"*Yum, pizza,*" said Connor. "I could eat three slices."
"I could eat *six* slices!" said Eddie.

Then it happened....

Gilbert started it—
the best pillow fight ever...

until Mr. Bellows stopped it!

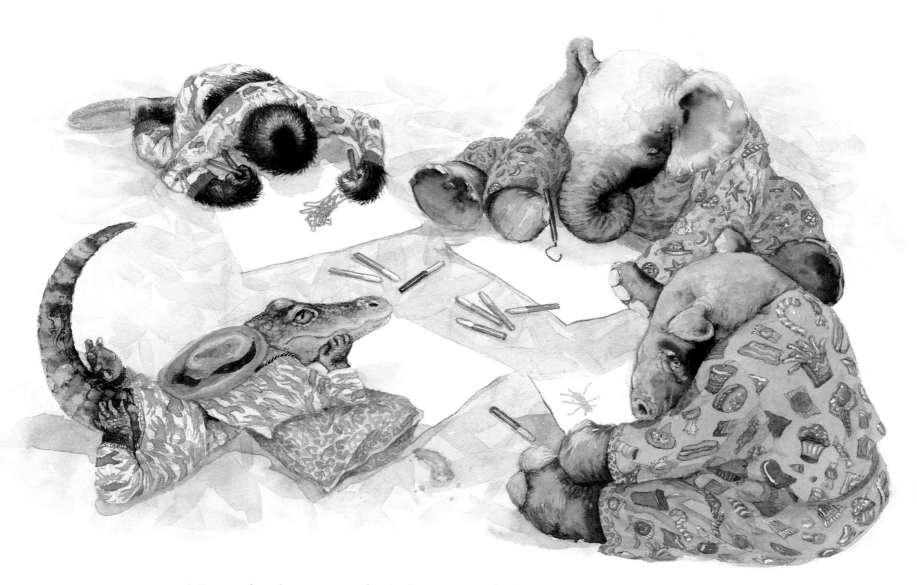

Next the boys settled down with big sheets of paper
and Eddie's new markers. Quietly, they began to draw.

"I love your circus picture," Ricky told Gilbert. "Can I have it?"
"No," Gilbert said. "I want to take it home to my mom."

Finally Mrs. Bellows called from the kitchen.
It was time to clean up.
"It's way past everyone's bedtime," she said.

The four friends washed and brushed.

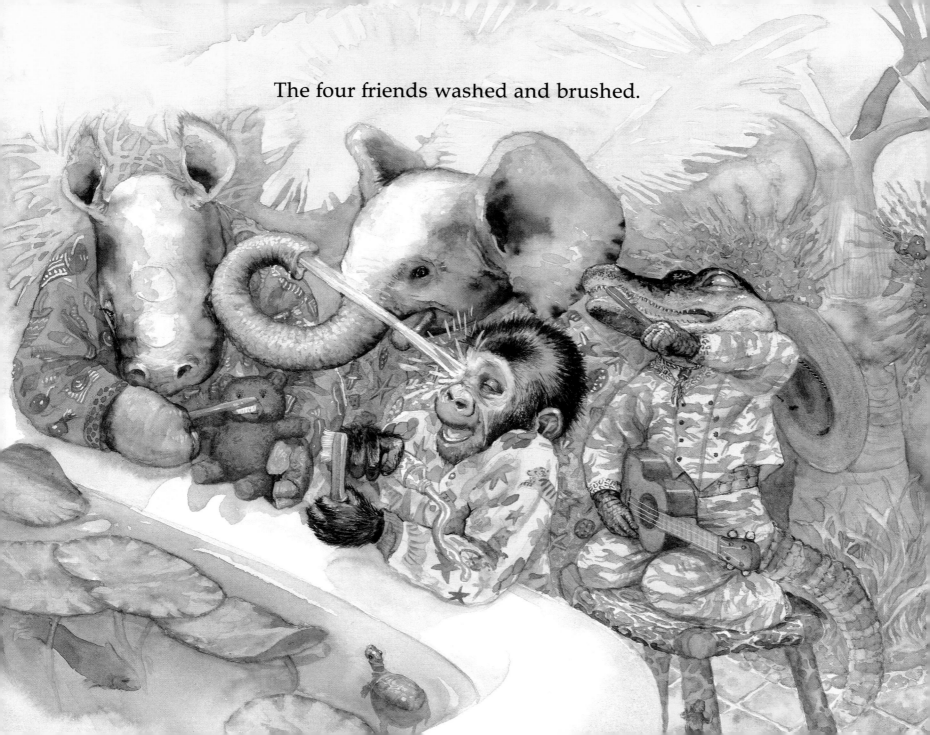

At last Conner, Eddie, Ricky, and Gilbert climbed into
their sleeping bags and snuggled down for the night.
But Gilbert couldn't fall asleep.

"I miss my mom," he whispered. "And I forgot to bring Clarence!" Gilbert tried not to cry, but a big tear rolled down his cheek.

No one knew what to do! Mrs. Bellows tried a glass of warm
milk and honey. Mr. Bellows tried to read a story.
But poor Gilbert just cried and cried.

Mrs. Bellows was about to call Gilbert's mom when suddenly
Conner had an idea. He picked up his ukelele and started to play
his favorite song. Eddie joined in, drumming on the pizza box,
and Ricky tapped on the wooden cups.

Then Ricky did
something special....

He gave Gilbert his teddy bear.
Gilbert hugged the bear close.
Within minutes, the boys
were fast asleep.

By morning, Gilbert was feeling just fine.

Mrs. Bellows brought in breakfast on a large tray.
The boys ate as they packed up their things.

Now it was Gilbert's turn to do something special.
He gave Ricky his circus picture. "I can draw another
one for my mom," he said.
"Thanks, Gilbert," said Ricky.

When the parents came to pick up their boys, Gilbert
said his thank-yous and good-byes.
Gilbert's mom gave him a hug. "I found Clarence at home
last night," she whispered. "Did you miss him?"
"I was okay, Mom," said Gilbert with a smile.
"I had my best friends!"